VIKING
Published by the Penguin Group
Penguin Putnam Books for Young Readers
345 Hudson Street, New York, New York 10014, U.S.A.
Penguin Books Ltd, Registered Offices: Harmondsworth, Middlesex, England

Published in 2001 by Viking, a division of Penguin Putnam Books for Young Readers

1 3 5 7 9 10 8 6 4 2

LIBRARY OF CONGRESS CATALOGING-IN-PUBLICATION DATA
Hutchins, H. J. (Hazel J.)
One dark night / by Hazel Hutchins ; illustrated by Susan Hartung.
p.   cm.
Summary: A young boy and his grandparents help a mother cat and her kittens
find safety during a summer thunderstorm.
ISBN 0-670-89246-7 (hardcover)
[1. Cats—Fiction. 2. Animals—Infancy—Fiction.
3. Thunderstorms—Fiction. 4. Grandparents—Fiction.]
I. Hartung, Susan Kathleen, ill. II. Title.
PZ7.H96162 On 2001
[E]—dc21
00–010534

Printed in Hong Kong • Set in Esprit
Book design by Teresa Kietlinski

The illustrations for this book were created using oil paint glazes
on sealed paper. The paint is blotted and manipulated
to create different effects.

For Wil
—H. H.

For Jim and Heide
—S. K. H.

One dark night,
lightning flashes.
Count the seconds before the thunder rolls.
One, two, three, four, five, six,
seven, eight, nine, ten.
Baroom!
A summer storm is two miles away
and coming closer.

Jonathan looks into the night.
Something small and dark is looking back at him.

He races downstairs and
throws open the screen door.
"The stray cat's afraid of the
thunder!" he tells his grandparents.
"Stray cats aren't afraid of storms,"
says Grandfather.
"Look out! I think she's got a
mouse!" cries Grandmother.
But stray cat is already inside
and laying her prize on the rug.

"It's a kitten!" says Jonathan.
One small kitten—soft as whispers, gray as dawn.

Lightning spills into the room.
Count the seconds before the thunder rolls.
One, two, three, four, five . . .
BAROOM!
The storm is one mile away
and coming closer.
Stray cat dashes out into the night.

"Come back!" calls Jonathan.
He steps into the brooding dark,
but Grandfather gently draws him inside
and pulls the screen door shut.

Jonathan lays his bathrobe on the rug.
He snuggles the kitten within its folds.
"We'll take care of it, won't we?" he asks.
"As ever best we can," says Grandmother.
But how can they take care of anything so small?

A scratching at the door.
Two green eyes peer in at them.
"She's back! She's back!" cries Jonathan
and races to the door.
Stray cat enters, carrying
a second kitten—soft as stuffing, white as snow.

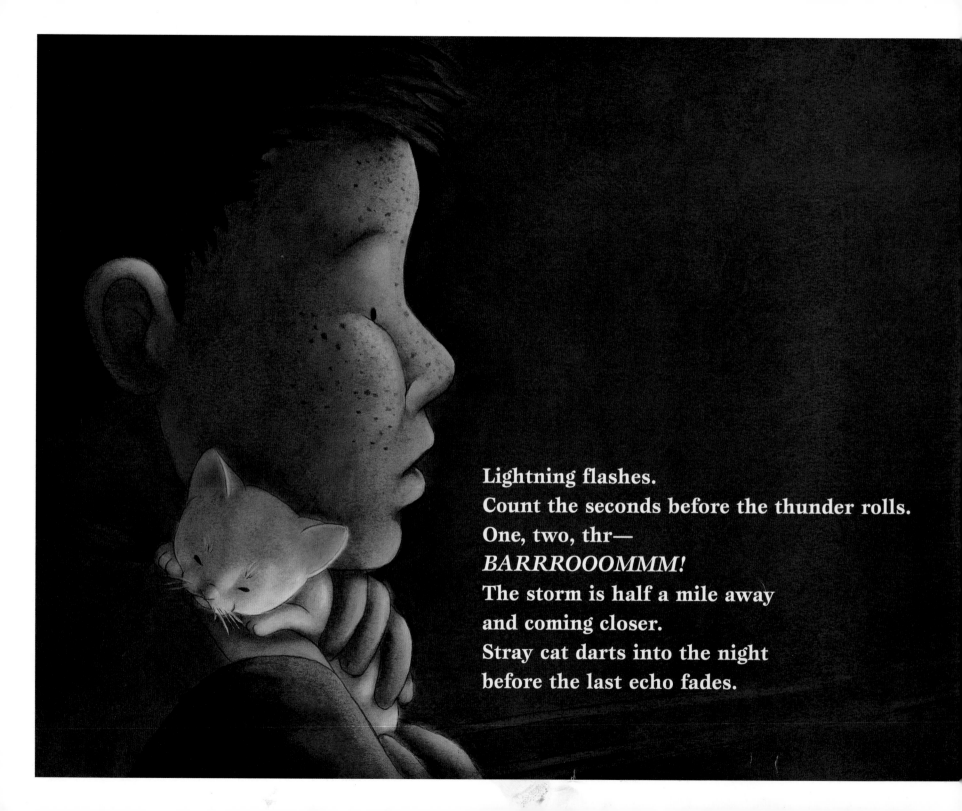

Lightning flashes.
Count the seconds before the thunder rolls.
One, two, thr—
BARRROOOMMM!
The storm is half a mile away
and coming closer.
Stray cat darts into the night
before the last echo fades.

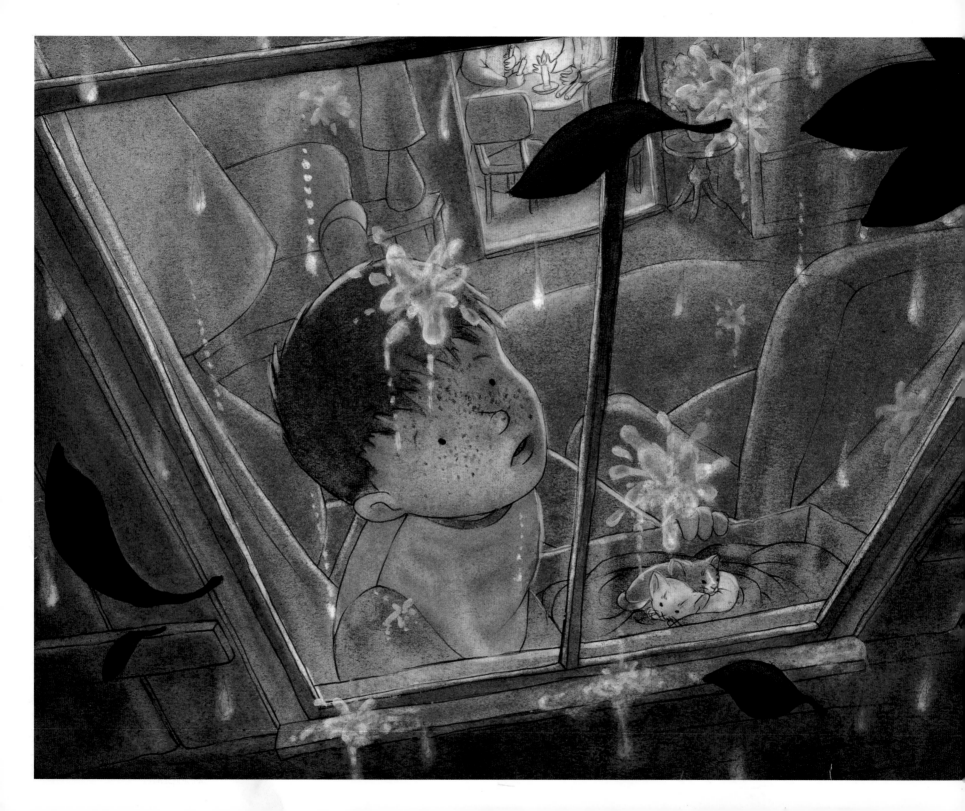

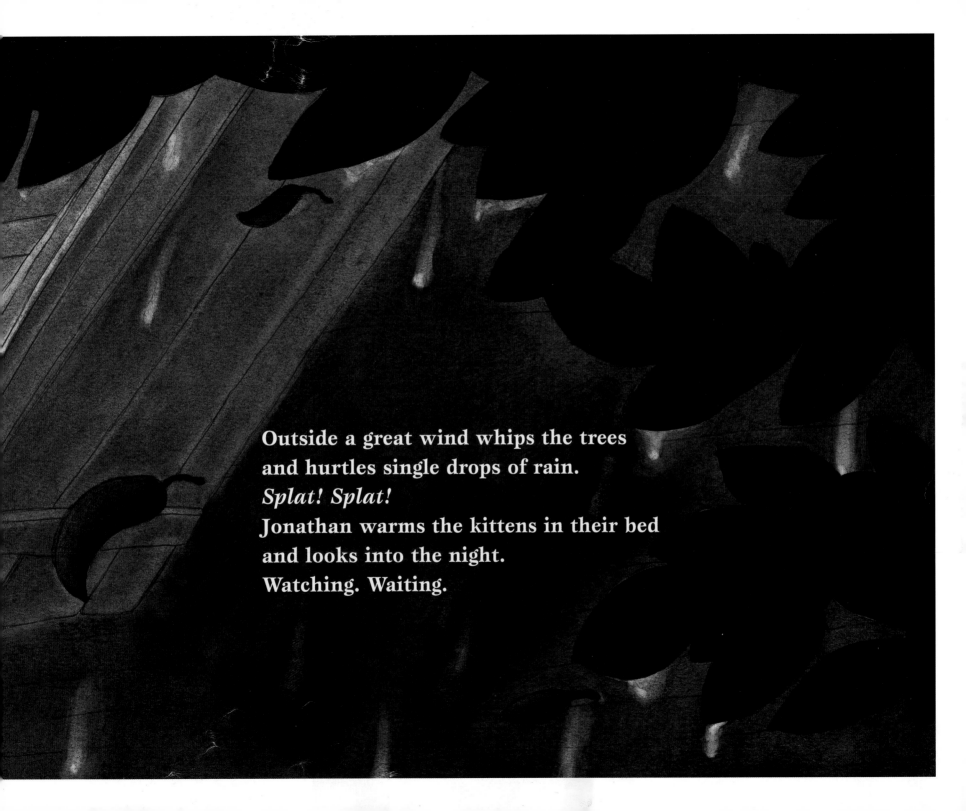

Outside a great wind whips the trees
and hurtles single drops of rain.
Splat! Splat!
Jonathan warms the kittens in their bed
and looks into the night.
Watching. Waiting.

This time when the lightning comes it splits the sky
with wild, white brightness.
There is no time to count before the thunder cracks.
BAAAARRRROOOOM!
A hard rain drums the roof
and pounds into the grass like something angry.
"There she is!" cries Jonathan.

The next moment he is outside too,
to help them battle through the rain.
One boy, one cat,
and a third small kitten—wet as water, black as night.

The rain pours.
Jonathan drips puddles on the floor.
"Are there any more?" he asks stray cat.
"Do we need another trip?"

But stray cat climbs into
the bathrobe, licking, nudging,
and arranging her family.

They are all here.
One stray cat
and three small kittens,
safe from the rain and the wind
and the rolling thunder,
safe with Jonathan,
safe with his grandparents,
one dark night.